Funny Bone Re...

MW00748256

The Lucky Day Picnic

by Barbara Bakowski • illustrated by Steve Cox

RED CHAIR •PRESS•

On the first day of summer,
Ricky Raccoon invited
his friends to a picnic.
They were delighted!

"Please come to the pond
on Friday at one.
Bring your favorite snack.
We'll have plenty of fun."

Sam Squirrel gathered walnuts,
his tastiest treat.
He imagined his friends
bringing more nuts to eat.

4

What was Beryl's best snack?
The bear had one wish.
Her big picnic pail
was piled high with fresh fish.

Lettuce and carrots made
a fine feast for Reggie.
The rabbit hopped to his yard
and filled baskets with veggies.

Robin Redbreast picked apples
and lots of red cherries.

She plucked purple grapes
and juicy blueberries.

As they packed picnic baskets,
each one of the guests
thought the others would bring
the same snack he liked best!

But the friends were surprised
at the table of treats.
For each guest had brought
something different to eat.

"A rainbow of snacks!
It's our lucky day!
From these healthy foods
we get energy to play."

So after their picnic,
they went for a swim.
And Ricky Raccoon
was first to jump in!

Big Question: What types of snacks can help you stay healthy and have energy to work and play?

Big Words:

gather: to collect

imagine: to form a picture in the mind

energy: the ability or power to do activities